pk 26/7/07

Who are you, Baby Kangaroo?

written by Stella Blackstone
illustrated by Clare Beaton

Barefoot Books
Celebrating Art and Story

'Who are you, baby kangaroo?'
'I'm not going to tell you. You'll have to ask...

...the wolf cubs.'
'Wolf cubs, wolf cubs, can you give me a clue?
Can you tell me the name of the baby kangaroo?'
'Oh no, we don't know. Why don't you ask...

...the cygnets?'
'Cygnets, cygnets, can you give me a clue?
Can you tell me the name of the baby kangaroo?'
'Oh no, we don't know. Why don't you ask...

'...the piglets?'
'Piglets, piglets, can you give me a clue?
Can you tell me the name of the baby kangaroo?'
'Oh no, we don't know. Why don't you ask...

…the penguin chicks?'

'Penguin chicks, penguin chicks, can you give me a clue?

Can you tell me the name of the baby kangaroo?'

'Oh no, we don't know. Why don't you ask…

'...the moose calves?'

'Moose calves, moose calves, can you give me a clue?

Can you tell me the name of the baby kangaroo?'

'Oh no, we don't know. Why don't you ask...

...the zebra foals?'
'Zebra foals, zebra foals, can you give me a clue?
Can you tell me the name of the baby kangaroo?'
'Oh no, we don't know. Why don't you ask...

…the tadpoles?'
'Tadpoles, tadpoles, can you give me a clue?
Can you tell me the name of the baby kangaroo?'
'Oh no, we don't know. Why don't you ask…

...the woolly lambs?'
'Woolly lambs, woolly lambs, can you give me a clue?
Can you tell me the name of the baby kangaroo?'
'Oh no, we don't know. Why don't you ask...

...the beaver kittens?'

'Beaver kittens, beaver kittens, can you give me a clue?

Can you tell me the name of the baby kangaroo?'

'Oh no, we don't know. Why don't you ask...

...his mother?'
'What a good idea!
Tell me, tell me, Mummy Kangaroo,
What is the name of your baby kangaroo?'

'You've travelled all around the world looking for a clue.
Your answer is not far away. My baby kangaroo is...

...a joey!
And tell me, little puppy, where's your mum, and who are you?'

'Here she comes to fetch me with my brothers, small and new.
Thank you for helping me, Mummy Kangaroo!'

The Animals and their Babies

Wolves – wolf cubs

(North America, Europe, Asia and the Arctic)

Wolves live together in families or packs that travel and hunt together. Usually just the leaders have cubs, but the whole pack helps to raise them. One litter of about three to six cubs is born every year in an underground den. While the mother is giving birth, the pack gathers outside and howls as each cub is born. Wolf cubs cannot see or hear when they are born but after a few weeks they are busily exploring outside. When the pack goes off to hunt, one wolf, called the aunt, stays behind to look after the cubs.

Swans – cygnets

(everywhere except Antarctica)

Swans mate for life, and build huge nests in safe places on the ground near water. They lay between three and eight pale, bluish-green eggs at a time. After they have hatched, the grey, furry cygnets are very helpless and keep close to their parents, even getting lifts on their backs. They learn to swim after a few days and start to fly when they are about four months old.

Pigs – piglets

(worldwide)

Mother pigs are called sows, and usually give birth twice a year to a litter of piglets numbering anything from six to twenty-five (the record is over thirty!) Sows lie down and grunt to let their piglets know when it is feeding time. The last piglet born is the smallest and is called the 'runt'. It often dies unless it is taken away from the rest of the litter and nursed by hand.

Penguins – penguin chicks
(Antarctica)

Penguins live by the sea in large groups called rookeries. They all have their babies at the same time of year. The penguins in this story are Emperor penguins. The female Emperor penguin lays a single egg which the male looks after for two months, keeping it warm on his feet. When the egg hatches the male goes off to feed while the female looks after the baby. Later they take it in turns to feed their chick. Penguin chicks take to the water after eight or nine weeks and form groups called 'crèches' to stay together for warmth and protection.

Moose – moose calves
(North America)

Moose are the world's largest deer. Moose cows usually give birth to twins, and sometimes triplets. Normally calm, quiet animals that avoid people, they can become very angry when protecting their young. The mother makes a long cough-like moaning sound to gather her calves to her. The calves stay with their mother for a year before becoming independent.

Zebras – zebra foals
(Africa)

A new zebra foal can stand up on its long wobbly legs fifteen minutes after being born. It must quickly learn to walk so that it can follow its mother away from danger. The mother will only give birth to one foal — twins are very rare. Zebra foals are born with a light brown background colour on their coats, instead of the white colour we see on adults. This helps to hide them from hungry lions and hyenas.

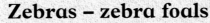

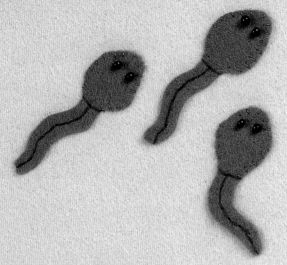

Frogs – tadpoles
(worldwide)

In the spring, frogs lay hundreds of eggs, called frogspawn, in ponds. After seven to fourteen days, the frogspawn turns into tadpoles. The tadpoles then grow legs, lose their tails and become tiny frogs. Now they are ready to leave the water and grow into adults on land. Many tadpoles get eaten by fish, birds and other animals and this is why so many eggs need to be laid.

Sheep – lambs
(worldwide)

Ewes (female sheep) normally give birth once a year, and have one to three lambs. The mother knows her lamb by its smell and the lamb recognises its mother by her bleat. Lambs are very playful and run and skip around the field together. Some newborn lambs are very weak and some are rejected by their mothers. These are taken indoors by the farmer's family and fed by bottle.

Beavers – beaver kittens
(North America)

Male and female beavers stay together for life. The mother usually has a litter of four or five kittens. They are born in a nest in the middle of a large pile of logs and stones, stuck together with mud, called a lodge. Beaver kittens are born with lots of fur and with their eyes open. They can get into the water as soon as half an hour after birth, and are skilful swimmers within a week. On land, their mother often carries them around on her broad tail as she walks. Young beavers stay with their families for about two years, then leave to build their own lodges.

Kangaroos – joeys

(Australia)

When joeys are born, they are very tiny — only 2.5cm long. Just one baby is born at a time. It crawls up the mother's pouch along a path the mother licks in her fur. Once in the pouch, the joey clings to a teat and drinks from this until it is about six months old. After leaving the pouch, it still returns to feed for another six months — running about with other joeys and jumping in and out of the pouch whenever it is hungry, frightened or tired.

Dogs – puppies

(worldwide)

Litters of puppies vary in size — the largest ever recorded was twenty-three puppies! Newborn puppies are completely dependent on their mothers. Like kittens, they are born with their eyes closed. Only their noses work immediately, sniffing for their mother's milk. For the first few weeks they feed and sleep, cuddling up together to keep warm. They are not colour blind, but see the world in the same way that we see it at twilight. Not all puppies are born in their adult colours. Dalmatian puppies only start getting their spots when they are about two weeks old.

for Natasha, Brendan and Noah — S. B.
for Joanna and her enthusiasm — C. B.

Barefoot Books
124 Walcot Street
Bath
BA1 5BG

This book was typeset in Plantin Schoolbook Bold 22 on 31 point
The illustrations were prepared in antique fabrics and felt
with sequins, buttons, beads and assorted bric-a-brac

Graphic design by Judy Linard, London
Colour separation by Bright Arts, Singapore
Printed and bound in Singapore by Tien Wah Press (Pte) Ltd

This book has been printed on 100% acid-free paper
ISBN 1-84148-216-1
British Cataloguing-in-Publication Data:
a catalogue record for this book is available from the British Library
1 3 5 7 9 8 6 4 2

Barefoot Books
Celebrating Art and Story

At Barefoot Books, we celebrate art and story
with books that open the hearts and minds of children
from all walks of life, inspiring them to read deeper,
search further, and explore their own creative gifts.
Taking our inspiration from many different cultures,
we focus on themes that encourage independence of
spirit, enthusiasm for learning, and acceptance of
other traditions. Thoughtfully prepared by writers,
artists and storytellers from all over the world, our
products combine the best of the present with the
best of the past to educate our children as the
caretakers of tomorrow.

www.barefootbooks.com